THE
MALTESE FELINE

OTHER MYSTERIES BY THE AUTHOR

Determined Detectives

The Phantom of the Operetta

Merger on the Orient Expressway

The Mysterious Case Case

Sebastian (Super Sleuth) and the
Bone to Pick Mystery

Sebastian (Super Sleuth) and the
Clumsy Cowboy

Sebastian (Super Sleuth) and the
Crummy Yummies Caper

Sebastian (Super Sleuth) and the
Hair of the Dog Mystery

Sebastian (Super Sleuth) and the
Purloined Sirloin

Sebastian (Super Sleuth) and the
Santa Claus Caper

Sebastian (Super Sleuth) and the
Secret of the Skewered Skier

Sebastian (Super Sleuth) and the
Stars-in-His-Eyes Mystery

DETERMINED DETECTIVES

THE
MALTESE FELINE

by Mary Blount Christian

illustrated by Kathleen Collins Howell

E. P. DUTTON   NEW YORK

Library of Congress Cataloging-in-Publication Data

Christian, Mary Blount.
    The Maltese feline.

    (Determined detectives)
    Summary: Fenton and Gerald investigate a suspected
kidnapping after finding a note containing a plea for
help tucked inside a cat's collar.
    [1. Mystery and detective stories] I. Howell, Kathleen,
Collins, ill. II. Title. III. Series: Christian, Mary
Blount. Determined Detectives.
PZ7.C4528Mal 1987 [Fic] 87-24367
ISBN 0-525-44334-7

Published in the United States by E. P. Dutton,
2 Park Avenue, New York, N.Y. 10016,
a division of NAL Penguin Inc.

Published simultaneously in Canada by
Fitzhenry & Whiteside Limited, Toronto

Printed in the U.S.A.   W   First Edition
10 9 8 7 6 5 4 3 2 1

for Jason, a Determined Reader

CONTENTS

Catastrophe!

I spread a glop of tuna fish across the bread and added a couple of dill pickle slices. There was a knock at the kitchen door—three rapid knocks, a pause, then two more. That was our secret signal, so I jammed the two pieces of bread together and yelled, "Come on in, Gerald!"

Gerald Grubbs is my junior partner in Smith and Grubbs, Determined Detectives. I, Fenton P. Smith, am his role model and idol, being a better sleuth. Since we were between cases at the moment, we had decided to go out for Little League baseball. The teacher had handed out the announcements before school was out. Mom thought I ought to be doing something "constructive" and "supervised" over vacation, and it's important to keep physically fit anyway. No telling when we might get involved in a marathon criminal chase or something that would stop anyone but the Determined Detectives.

"Hurry," Gerald said. "Tryouts will start in ten minutes." He sniffled. Gerald always sniffles when he is nervous, and Gerald is almost always nervous about something.

We were out of plastic bags, so I wrapped my sandwich in a napkin and shoved it into a paper sack along with an apple and a banana. The coach had said he would furnish the drinks.

I grabbed my lunch and my baseball glove and scooted out the back door behind Gerald, pausing to listen for the lock to click shut. "The park's only a couple of blocks; we'll make it in plenty of time," I assured him. "I just hope you-know-who isn't trying out, too."

I was talking about dumb old Mae Donna Dockstadter. She's a big pain, always trying to butt in on our mystery cases, following us around and bragging about herself. Yuk! If it wasn't for her father . . . Mae Donna let it slip one time: He's a secret agent. What a guy!

He's always talking in riddles, calling the bad guys vermin. His cover is a pest exterminator. What a great way to be able to slip into houses and spy on people and stuff. Who'd ever suspect? Even knowing the truth, I've sometimes had my doubts about him—that's how good he is. He's advised the Determined Detectives a few times, and his suggestions really worked. So, in appreciation, I don't tell his daughter what a jerk she is—well, not often, anyway.

I decided to shove such an unpleasant thought as

Mae Donna from my mind. I noticed that Gerald was carrying a large bag. Detectives, especially the good ones like myself, tend to notice anything unusual. "Whatcha got there, Gerald?" I asked. "Your family's groceries for the week?"

"My lunch, of course," Gerald replied. "I have to keep up my energy if I'm gonna be running the bases."

I tactfully swallowed my laughter. "Well, first you gotta hit the ball," I said. Gerald isn't as good a player as I am. "And if you eat so much you can't see the ball for your stomach, you won't need to run much."

Gerald shrugged. "I'd rather be snooping around some mystery anyway."

I nodded. So would I. But then our town, Scudder, is kind of small. It's pretty quiet most of the time; you have to look hard to find mysteries. Gerald and I figured it would be nice if some of the big cities would export a few criminals, since they've got so many to spare. But I guess it doesn't really work that way.

The park was just ahead. It was a whole square block, named after the mother of some lady that gave the property to the city—Millie Collinbacher Park. The Collinbacher house, a big old red brick mansion, was across the street behind a high brick fence with locked iron gates.

"Look," Gerald said, pointing toward the park. "A whole bunch of kids are already there trying out."

The coach, Travis Laurence, was on the pitcher's mound, tossing balls over home plate. Kids were lined up, taking turns at bat. One stepped up to the plate and

3

crouched, waiting. Then *whack!* the bat connected and the ball went whizzing past the coach into center field.

"Not bad," I said. But then the kid's cap slid back, and I could see a headful of rusty slinkies—red hair sproinging out in every direction. "Oh, no!" I moaned. Our day had definitely just taken a turn for the worse; it was dumb old Mae Donna Dockstadter.

Gerald and I got in the line. I slunk down, trying to keep the kids in front of me between myself and Mae Donna, who was strutting around as if she'd been voted into the Baseball Hall of Fame.

Too late. She spotted me. "A good solid hit to center field," she bragged. "Just another one of my many talents." Her little green cat-eyes glistened like beads. "Top that, if you can." She smirked, and her zillions of freckles seemed to run together. She tossed her head so her iodine-colored curls flip-flopped, and then she flounced off before I could answer.

I curled my upper lip, mumbling under my breath. The line moved along until it was my time at bat. I spread my feet apart and squinted toward the pitcher's mound. Coach Laurence threw one over the plate. The sun must have got in my eyes at that very moment, because I swung the bat but barely connected with the ball. It rolled halfway between home plate and the pitcher's mound and then stopped dead. I felt the blood rush to my face as I left the plate.

Mae Donna was lounging under the tree where she had her dog tied up. Now she reached into a big floppy purse at her side and pulled out a magnifying glass. "Let

4

me see that one again!" she teased, holding the glass up to her eye. "Wow, Slammer Smith strikes again!"

"It was a bunt!" I yelled at her.

"I saw you, weirdo," she said, her little cat-eyes dancing. "You swung wide and hard. You just missed it, that's what. The ball only accidentally ran into your bat."

"It takes talent to make people *think* you're going to hit one to the outfield and then bunt it, Mae Donna," I argued. "You'd never be able to do that!"

I slumped onto the bench, waiting for Gerald to have his turn. Gerald hit a ground ball down the line just inside first base. Fortunately *he* was too good a friend to brag.

What a turn of events. One little fluff and I was probably going to be kept off the team. What was worse, Mae Donna was going to make it! Well, I'd rather be sleuthing than playing ball any day. And who wanted to be on a team with dumb old Mae Donna.

The coach complimented us—*all* of us—and told us to come back next Monday afternoon, when he'd assign positions. I felt relieved that I'd be on the team and have another chance to show how good I was.

"Lunchtime!" the coach yelled. He waved us toward a picnic table where there were plastic cups and a big thermos the coach had brought.

I poured myself some of the cherry drink and found a spot under a pine tree. Gerald joined me. Kids scattered around on the ground eating whatever they'd brought.

Fortunately Mae Donna ate her lunch under the tree with her dog and didn't try to join us. She probably knew her dog liked her better than we did. She called her dog Stew because it was such a mixture of breeds. It looked as if it had on a fur suit about two sizes too big that sort of hung in wrinkles around its feet and forehead. The dog was okay—it was the *owner* that was a pest.

I couldn't eat my whole tuna sandwich, so I threw the rest of it in my sack. Gerald looked longingly at it. "I'll finish it later," I told him. No need in keeping his hopes up.

He sniffled.

"Let's get out of here before Mae Donna decides to follow us," I whispered.

We walked along Collinbacher Boulevard slowly, letting our lunches settle. Suddenly I had this creepy feeling we were being followed. "Hold it," I whispered to Gerald. A good detective, such as myself, has this sort of sixth sense. I glanced back over my shoulder.

The street looked empty. I sniffed—no icky odor of lavender perfume. Mae Donna wears enough of it to drown in, but she can never figure out how I know when she's skulking around spying on us. "Come on," I said to Gerald. "It seems safe enough."

We moved on, but I just couldn't shake the feeling that we were not alone.

Meooooow.

I whirled around to see a pudgy cat with short, dark bluish hair and orange eyes. It was standing on the sidewalk about three feet behind us, its tail flicking back and forth. It lifted its nose to sniff my sack. There was a look of pure delight on its face.

"It smells your tuna fish sandwich," Gerald said. "Poor little kitty, it must be lost and hungry."

"Little!" I said. "It looks a-cat-and-a-half wide to me."

"Maybe it just has fat fur," Gerald argued. I could tell he was on the side of anybody or anything that liked to eat.

It did seem sort of lost, though. I'd never seen it around here before. But hungry? It looked too plump and well fed to be really starving. Still, what cat could resist tuna?

The cat curled around my pant leg, purring like a diesel motor.

I bent down and stroked its head. Then I pulled out the leftover half of my sandwich and broke it into little pieces. The cat sniffed quickly, then choked down the tuna, leaving the pickles.

Suddenly the cat bristled, its orange eyes flashing like the lights on a patrol car. I looked up to see Mae Donna and Stew coming toward us fast. Stew must have spotted the poor cat, and was barreling down on it. Mae Donna's eyes were all bugged out like a frog's, and she was holding on to Stew's leash with both hands, pulling with all her might. But the dog was dragging her along easily.

I moved to throw myself between the dog and the cat, but the cat would have none of that. Instead, it swelled up like a blimp, its fur standing out stiff and straight. Its claws sprang out like daggers. *Pffftttt!* It spat angrily.

Stew did a quick U-turn and skittered around behind Mae Donna's legs, peering out, his eyes glassy with fear.

Mae Donna started yelling. "Stew, didn't you hear me tell you to heel? Shame! Shame!" I figured she was madder at her dog for being such a coward than for chasing a cat.

I swelled with pride. That kitty had bluffed Mae Donna's big old dog. What a tough cat! Maybe all that fat was pure muscle! And it was obviously lost, poor thing. Why else would it follow a couple of strange kids—make that *unknown* kids. "I guess the least I can do is to take you home with me until I find out who you belong to," I said.

I scooped the cat into my arms, and that was when I noticed the collar it was wearing. It was really fancy, with colored glass cut to look like rubies and diamonds. The glass stones were fixed in a flower design so it seemed like the cat had a wreath of daisies around its neck. And then I saw something stuck in the collar—a rolled up piece of paper.

I pulled it out and unfolded it. Scribbled in red crayon was a note that said, *Help me, please!*

◈◈◈◈◈◈◈◈◈

Catalog of Clues

I felt the hair on my neck stand up. I cleared my throat and tried to hide the excitement in my voice.

"This calls for action by the Determined Detectives. This cat is a messenger from somebody in distress. But who?"

"It's probably a joke!" Mae Donna said, looking over my shoulder. "The note isn't even signed. What kind of person would ask for help and not tell you who or where?" She scrounged around in her purse and pulled out a jar of dark powder. "Maybe we should take finger-prints—just in case."

I glared at her and held the note out of reach. Who had asked her to join our investigation anyway? I mean, it was *my* tuna that attracted the cat in the first place! "Don't be dumb, Mae Donna. If we got fingerprints, what would we have? We have nothing to compare them to. Criminals have fingerprints on file, not victims." I studied the note. "It looks like somebody tried to sign it. See?" I held the note out so Mae Donna and Gerald could see. "It's kind of a half moon—but that could be the start of an *O* or a *C* or a *Q* or even a *G* or maybe an *A* or *S*. Whoever wrote this was probably interrupted before he or she could sign it."

"See if the cat's vaccination tags are attached to the collar," Mae Donna said. "We can trace the owner through the veterinarian."

I didn't like the sound of that *we* in there. Mae Donna was already horning in, trying to solve our case. What was worse, she was right. The tags would be the fastest, most perfect way to find out who wrote the note. Of course, I'd have thought of that myself in another second.

I checked the cat's collar. "No tags," I said. "Any more ideas?" I looked right at Gerald and ignored Mae Donna, hoping she'd get mad and leave.

"We should take the note to the sheriff," Gerald said. "Maybe he can find fingerprints on it or something."

"The sheriff would say it was probably a joke," said Mae Donna. "It's written in crayon. He'd just think one of us or some other kid was pulling a prank. I remember one time I . . ."

"Yeah," I said, interrupting her before she went off into one of her boring adventures. "You're right. He'd just throw us out. It's probably just some kid playing around." I didn't think that for one minute, but I didn't want Mae Donna hanging around while we worked on a case.

11

I sniffed the paper. It didn't smell exactly like crayon. It had a sweeter smell, but I couldn't quite place it.

"Let's knock on doors around here," Mae Donna suggested. "Cats don't stray too far from their houses. We can just ask everybody if it's their cat."

I looked up and down the street. There were plenty of houses—mansions, really. This was the richest street in Scudder. The cat could have come from any one of them. Or maybe somebody had shoved it out of a car.

"Dumb idea, Mae Donna," I said. "The message asks for *help.* That means trouble. What if the wrong person, the one that is causing the trouble, answered the door? Then *we'd* need help, too!"

She shrugged. "Whatever."

I undid the fancy collar and took it off the cat. Instead of buckling like most collars I'd seen, it had a snap clasp. "It's an unusual collar. Maybe the collar was bought in a pet store nearby. Maybe the clerk would remember selling it," I said. I turned the collar over. There was a name engraved on it. *MAC.* "So that's your name, huh, kitty? Mac. Okay, Mac. I'll get you to my house, and we'll figure out what to do."

Meooow, Mac said. I took that for okay.

"Perhaps I haven't mentioned this before," Mae Donna said, her nose in the air, "but I am something of an animal expert. I shall be glad to share my vast knowledge. . . ."

"Can it, Mae Donna," I said. "Just because you are an animal and you've read Kipling's *Jungle Book* doesn't make you an animal *expert.* Why don't you

just take your dog home before Mac here decides to beat him up again."

As if on cue, Mac gave one last hiss, just to show who was in charge.

"Humph!" Mae Donna said, turning her back to us. She stalked off with old Stew, who seemed glad to get away from Mac. "If I wanted to study animal behavior, I'd just need to watch *you*. What I read was my uncle's veterinary books," she yelled over her shoulder. "And *I* happen to know what kind of a cat you have there— just in case you're interested. Of course, I guess you already know that, don't you, Mr. Smarty?"

I *didn't* know, but I wasn't going to tell *her* that. If Mae Donna could find out, so could I. I stuck the rhinestone collar and note in my pocket and carried Mac the few blocks to my house.

Mom was still at work, so I got Mac a saucer of milk, which he lapped up right away. "I'll put Mac in my room," I told Gerald. "It might be better if Mac isn't the first thing Mom spots when she gets home."

Gerald followed me into my room, and we watched as Mac mewed and purred and curled up in the middle of my bed, staring at me with his big orange eyes.

"Oh, Mac," Gerald said, "if only you could talk."

Mac blinked. *Mrrrrrt.*

"I have a feeling that Mac *is* talking," I told Gerald. "We just don't understand the language."

"Maybe if we knew the kind of cat he is it would help," Gerald said, echoing my thoughts. "Owners of the same breed might know each other, especially if they belong to special breed clubs or show their cats. You know, like stamp collectors belong to clubs, or people with Ford Edsels hang out together. Maybe we should ask Mae Donna."

"I'd rather give up the detective business than ask her," I snarled. Sometimes I worry about Gerald. How could he even *think* such a thing? Asking Mae Donna for help was the last thing I wanted to do.

I looked at the cat with a detective's eye. Maybe twenty-nine inches from ears to tip of tail; maybe eight inches high and about a-cat-and-a-half wide. Bluish gray hair about as long as the last joint of my little finger. Orange eyes. Ordinary but kind of special looking.

"We'll go to the library and look in a cat book," I said.

"Library's closed," Gerald reminded me. "It's got short hours because of budget cuts, remember?"

"We can go tomorrow morning," I said.

"Tomorrow's Saturday. It'll be closed all day because—"

"Of the budget cuts," I finished. "Then we'll ask the pet store people. They ought to know."

"Bet it's already closed for the day," Gerald said, checking his watch. "And bet you it's only open Monday through Friday, too."

"You aren't making this any easier," I said. I decided to swallow my pride. "Okay, Gerald. Mom will be home any second, and I've got to build a case for keeping Mac around a few days. But first thing tomor-

15

row we'll see if the pet store is open. We'll try and find a vet—preferably no kin to you-know-who. If all else fails, we'll go see Mae Donna."

The door slammed and Mom called, "I'm home, Fenton!"

"And I'm gone!" Gerald whispered. "Good luck!"

I had a feeling I was going to need it.

◇◇◇◇◇◇◇◇◇

The Cat's
Out of the Bag

Gerald slipped out the front door, and I hunted up Mom's slippers—the fuzzy pink ones with the soft lining—and took them to her. "Hi, Mom!" I greeted her cheerily. "How was your day? I bet you're ready to slip out of your high heels and into these, aren't you?"

Mom wiggled her toes, oohing as she slid her feet into the slippers. Then she sort of snapped to attention and narrowed her eyes suspiciously. "Are you in trouble at school, Fenton?"

"School's out for the summer, Mom, remember?" I said. "That's a nice dress you have on."

"It's five years old, Fenton, and you've seen it hundreds of times." She put her hands on her hips and stared at me, one eyebrow raised. "Did you break a neighbor's window? Or run through their flowers with your bike? Or . . ."

"Mom!" I said. "Nothing like that at all! I've been a model child, honest."

Mom went into the kitchen and got out the spaghetti sauce, so I grabbed the package of pasta and put it on the kitchen counter. "Er, Mom, have you read that newest test in *Woman's Way* magazine?"

My mom is always taking those magazine tests, like "Is Your Child Going To Grow Up Right?" and "Is Your Marriage Really Happy or Do You Only Think It Is?" and dumb stuff like that.

She put her apron on and pulled a pound of ground meat from the fridge. She crumbled it into the skillet to brown. "I haven't had a chance yet. What did it say, Fenton?"

I figured I had her attention. "The test this month is called 'Can a Pet Really Help You Live Longer and More Healthfully?' "

"Now, Fenton, you know how I feel about having a pet with nobody here all day to look after it." The meat began to sizzle, and she stirred. "*Can* it? *Can* a pet help you live longer and more healthfully?"

"Oh, absolutely!" I said. I could tell she was really interested now. "Kids behave better, grown-ups feel less depressed and everybody is a lot nicer. The article said that they are even putting pets in mental hospitals and nursing homes. Everybody feels better with pets around."

She poured the sauce over the meat and lowered the heat. Then she eyed me from under frowning brows. "My instincts tell me this is another of your kooky

18

schemes, Fenton. I don't know . . . Maybe we should think about it, though. I'll check into the pet shops and ask pet owners. We wouldn't want to make a mistake. It's a shame you have to commit yourself before you really know how it will . . ."

"That's the funny part, Mom!" I said. "This really neat, exceptionally nice little cat followed me home today, sort of, and I'd like to—"

"Fenton!" she said as she slammed the lid down on the skillet. "A stray cat? That's dangerous. Why it could be rabid or—"

"No, Mom!" I argued. "This little cat belongs to somebody. It had on an expensive collar, so I'm sure the owner's the kind who would give the cat the proper shots and all. It's just temporary, Mom, until I find the owner. It'd be a good experiment to see if we really want a pet, honest!"

I ran and got Mac. I shoved him into Mom's arms, and he set up a loud purr. I could see Mom melting right before my eyes. She began to stroke his fur. "Well, I guess it won't hurt to keep him, just until you find his owner," she said. Mac touched his little black nose to her cheek and Mom laughed. "Okay, I'm convinced. I feel healthier already!" Mom narrowed her eyes at me. "But I want you to get started right away looking for the owner. Somebody is probably heartbroken at this very moment. Are you sure they don't go home if they're turned loose? You know, like horses to the barn?"

I wasn't ready to tell Mom my suspicions. She'd

19

probably get all upset and tell me to turn it over to the police. Or she'd just think I was being weird. I nodded with more enthusiasm than I felt. "Sure, Mom. Notices in the supermarket and the neighborhood newspaper ought to get the owner's attention." And maybe the kidnapper, too. I figured to stall the public notices until we'd had a chance to investigate a bit.

Mom called Dad, and he picked up some cat food and some litter and a litter box on his way home from work. Mac spent the evening cozying up to us, then settled down on my bed to sleep.

I put his rhinestone collar in my toy box. That was the safest place for a valuable clue. Who'd ever think to look among all that stuff? Somehow it didn't seem right to put something that fancy on a tough little fighter like Mac. I mean, he practically beat up Stew single-handedly—or is that single-pawed?

Before I went to bed, I pulled out the help note and looked at it again, turning it over and over in my hands. It wasn't notebook paper or anything cheap. It was pale blue and thick. It looked pretty expensive—like Mac's rhinestone collar.

I studied the words again. *Help me, please!* and that little curlicue that might be the beginning of somebody's name. If I were in immediate danger, what would I say? I wondered. Wouldn't I say, "Help" and give the address? But this said, "Help *me*" and even added "please." The person who wrote this was polite. And there was a comma between me and please.

Someone who stops to punctuate a plea for help

couldn't be in immediate danger, right? But then why would anyone send a message asking for help?

Mom yelled for me to turn off the light and go to bed. I put the note away and fell asleep with old Mac curled up on my chest.

When I woke up Mac was gone. I dashed out of my bedroom, yelling, "Mac! Here, kitty-kitty!"

I found him in the kitchen. He was sound asleep, curled up in Mom's lap while she read the morning paper. She was stroking him and grinning from ear to ear. Maybe pets really can make you feel healthier and happier.

Mom made a shushing gesture so I wouldn't wake up Mac, then wiggled her finger, motioning for me to come closer.

She planted a big kiss on my cheek. I blushed. "Aw, Mom," I said, wiping the lipstick from my face. My fingers brushed past my nose, and I sniffed. I sniffed again. It was a sweet odor—like a rose garden, maybe. "Mom, you're the greatest!" I yelled, running back to my room.

I grabbed the help note and sniffed it again. Sure enough, it was the same smell. That was it! It wasn't crayon the note was written in; it was lipstick. Some lady in Scudder was in trouble, and she had sent Mac to get help.

◆◇◆◇◆◇◆◇◆

Cat and Mouse

I fed Mac his breakfast and took a picture of him with
my instant camera. I figured a snapshot would be easier
to carry around than old Mac, who seemed to be even
fatter and lumpier this morning than yesterday.

I ate my own breakfast and settled Mac down for a
nice catnap in my room—this time on top of my dresser.
Then I looked in the phone book under pet stores and
veterinarians. There was only one pet store—Scudder is
a pretty small town—and it was closed for the weekend.
There were three veterinarians, including one named
Dockstadter. One was on the far side of town. And one
was closed on the weekend. That left the one named
Dockstadter, but I figured maybe he was more like his
brother than his niece. By that time Gerald had arrived.

I paced back and forth, stroking my chin the way I'd
seen detectives do on television. "This is what we've got
so far," I told Gerald. "I believe that somewhere in

Scudder there is a lady who is polite and grammatical, and she is in no immediate danger but is probably being held against her will."

Gerald stared wide-eyed at me. "You sound like Sherlock Holmes! How'd you figure out all that? You finally get Mac to talk?"

"And you sound like Watson," I said, grinning. "Elementary, dear Gerald. I feel sure it is a lady, because the note was written in lipstick on fancy stationery. The lady is polite and grammatical, because she said please and she used all the right punctuation. She is in no immediate danger, because she took the time to be polite and grammatical. And she is being held against her will, or she would have delivered the message herself instead of sending it by a cat, who could probably slither away, unnoticed by dastardly kidnappers."

I basked in Gerald's admiration for a moment, and then confessed, "But I still don't know anything about Mac. I wish we had all those FBI resources like Mr. Dockstadter has. The pet store is closed. One vet is closed, and another is across town," I said. "It looks like we are going to have to talk to Mae Donna's uncle. I guess that's better than talking to *her.*"

"Let's walk south on our street," I suggested. "Then we can cut over to Dockstadter's. Maybe we'll get lucky and see some grubby old kidnapper out yelling for Mac." We didn't see anybody, but just as we crossed Collinbacher I spotted something that made my pulse race. It was a van with a big plastic bug on top. The bug's feet and antennae were wiggling in the breeze. "Mr. Dockstadter!" I said. "Gerald, we're saved! Mr.

Dockstadter knows all kinds of neat stuff. He probably knows all about cats, too!"

Mae Donna's father was just getting out of his van with a great big spray can strapped to his back. "Hi!" I yelled. "Mr. Dockstadter, it's me, Fen—"

He slapped a cap over his kinky red hair and grinned. "Why, yes, Ferdy, how are you? And Gerhard."

"Fenton and Gerald," I said. "You'll remember, sir, that we're— er"—I choked on the words—"friends of Mae Donna's."

"Of course, Fermin," he said. "I remember. How can I forget two young men who want to follow in my humble footsteps. It's good to know that the next generation will be as dedicated to ridding this world of vermin as I have been."

I thought for a minute he might salute or something. "Uh, speaking of vermin, sir, could you offer us any advice on looking for them?"

Mr. Dockstadter nodded solemnly. "Fletcher, no home is spared—none. Vermin are in even the richest and best of them. It's a never ending battle, my boy."

"Even houses on Collinbacher Boulevard?" I asked. It would be hard to imagine spies and other bad guys there.

"Even here, Frelich," he said. "That's why I'm here right now."

"We won't breathe a word of it," I promised. He knew so much, I decided to chance it. I took out the picture of Mac. "Would you happen to know what kind of a cat this is, sir?"

He studied the picture. "Ahhh," he said. "A competitor in the vermin-busting business. Hmmmmm, I don't know one from the other, but my brother would know. He's a veterinarian."

"Yes, sir," I said. "We know—"

Mr. Dockstadter nodded. "His office is three blocks south and one west of here. Good luck, Fermin. You too, Gerik."

Before I could tell him we knew where his brother's office was, too, Mr. Dockstadter went into one of the houses on Collinbacher Boulevard. I motioned to Gerald to come.

We hiked on over to Murray Street and saw the sign—David Dockstadter, D.V.M. Small Animal Practice.

We went inside. And wouldn't you know? Who's the first person we see there but Mae Donna, her hair looking like a convention of hot dogs and her green eyes glaring at us. She was patting old Stew's head while he waited for his turn, quivering like a bowl of jelly. "Which of you animals is seeing my uncle?" Mae Donna said, smirking.

"We are merely here to confirm our findings regarding Mac," I said, trying to out–Mae Donna Mae Donna.

"What findings?" Gerald asked, sniffling. "I thought we came here because we didn't know anything." There are some days I regret having made Gerald my partner.

Mae Donna grinned. "Ha! I thought so! I knew you needed my expertise."

I searched my mind for something—anything—that

would put a lid on Mae Donna's mouth. "We ran into your father this morning," I said. That was always good for a tinge of red around the ears.

She flushed right on schedule. "You didn't!"

"Sure," I said, "and he offered us some timely advice."

Her green cat-eyes grew as big as saucers. "You talked to him about detective work!"

"We professionals have to stick together," I said, grinning.

A guy with red, tight curly hair and green eyes stuck his head out a door. "Ready for Stew's shot, Mae Donna?" he asked.

Stew sort of melted onto the floor, whimpering and rolling his eyes toward the door as if he were begging Mae Donna for mercy. I could've told him she'd never go for it. Mae Donna turned to us. "You might as well come in with me. Uncle David, these two nerds are in my class, and they want to ask you something. Can they come in with us?"

I narrowed my eyes at her, but turned back to give Dr. Dockstadter a reassuring smile.

"Sure," he said. "It'll probably take all of us to hold Stew down while he gets his shot, poor coward."

Mae Donna flushed a bright pink, and I smirked, thinking of brave old Mac. He probably didn't flinch at the veterinarian's.

We helped lift old Stew up on the table, and Dr. Dockstadter examined his eyes, his mouth and ears and checked his heartbeat. Then he got a needle and stuck it in the fleshy part of the poor dog's neck.

Stew squirmed, and I didn't feel so good either.

"It's all over. He's safe from rabies for another year. You can set him down now," Dr. Dockstadter said. "Now what brings you boys along with my niece?"

"We aren't really with—that is, we came sep—that is, do you recognize this cat? His name is Mac."

Dr. Dockstadter studied the picture. "Mac, you say? I don't have any patients with that name, but this looks like a Maltese. Maybe you could check with one of the state cat owners' organizations. Maybe the owner has registered it for shows. I can't recall any members right offhand, but it seems to me that they had a cat show here recently. Maybe the *Scudder Times* would have something about it."

We thanked him and left. Mae Donna had to take Stew home, so we didn't have to worry about her following us to the newspaper. All I had to worry about was Mr. Saxet. He gets a little upset when he sees me coming. It's just that disastrous things sort of happen when I'm around the newspaper office, and for some weird reason, he blames me.

I sent Gerald inside the office first to see if Mr. Saxet was there.

Gerald poked his head out and sniffled. "Coast is clear," he said, waving me in. "He's out on a story."

The newspaper had a cross-reference file where we could look up stories by subject or by the date they had appeared. We went to the *C* file and looked up cats. I read off the descriptions: Cat rescued from tree by the Scudder Fire Department; Cat given credit card by mistake; Cat gives birth to record litter; Cat show hits

28

kathleen collins howell

town; and Cat champion with trophy. "Cat shows—that's what we're looking for. According to this there should be a story in the April 10 issue on page three and another on April 17 on page one," I said, reading the dates by the cat show stories.

I asked the newspaper librarian for the clippings.

"We don't keep clippings anymore—they take up too much storage space," he said. "We put all the past issues on microfilm. April is complete. The film is labeled by the month." He pointed us to a machine. "Load the spool on the left side. It feeds onto the empty spool on the right of the machine. Then just push the blue button until you find the day and page you're looking for.

"The screen shows only about a quarter of a page, but you can move the little lever up and down to scan the page for the article you want. If you want a copy of a story, you just center it on the screen and push this red button. It will give you a printout. And don't forget to rewind the film and return it to me. Mr. Saxet gets downright upset if any of it is left out."

I sure didn't want to upset Mr. Saxet, but it all sounded simple enough. We stuck the film reel on the machine, threaded the film onto the empty spool and pushed the blue button. Days glided past on the little screen. April 1, 2, 3 . . . I eased up on the button as April 9 passed, and there was April 10. I stopped the machine on page three and found the story in the bottom left corner of the page. I could read the headline: CAT SHOW HITS TOWN OF SCUDDER. But the story was too hard to read, because it was all negative on the screen.

I pushed the red button. The machine buzzed and whirred, and a printout came out, this time a positive black and white. I could read the story, but the picture was too dark and smudged to see clearly. I found the April 17 article and made a printout.

Gerald read the first article aloud. "It says that cats of all breeds were in the show. And the words under this picture we can't see names a cat. Hey, it says it's a Maltese named Cleopatra of Cornwall."

"Maybe that owner might know something about Mac and his owner," I suggested. "We could ask." I read the caption under the picture. " 'Cleopatra is owned by Miss Mary Alice Collinbacher'—hey, that's the lady who gave the park where we're going to play baseball. That big old red brick mansion is hers. We know right where she lives—no problem."

"Gee," Gerald said. "It's a shame the picture didn't turn out nice. People always like getting extra copies of their pictures. She'd probably appreciate it so much she'd be willing to help, don't you think?"

That wasn't a bad idea, considering it was Gerald's. "Maybe we can ask the photographer that took it. It says here that it was Leroy Lambert. He might have an extra copy or something. But Gerald," I warned, "be careful in the photography lab. We mustn't touch anything or Mr. Saxet will really be mad."

We found Mr. Lambert in the lab. He was printing up some pictures. "Cat show, Mary Alice Collinbacher? Oh, sure, I have an extra picture or two of that in the file." He led us into the next room and rummaged through a drawer. He pulled out a couple of pictures and stuck them in an envelope for us. "Here you go, boys."

We took the envelope and thanked Mr. Lambert. "Oh, brother!" I said as we were leaving the lab. "I forgot to rewind and return the film. I better get that done before Mr. Saxet comes back and catches me here."

We hurried back to the microfilm machine, and I pushed the red rewind button. *Brrrrrrt!* Film rolled off the right spool, okay. But it sure wasn't feeding back on the left one. Film snaked into piles and across the floor. "How do you stop this thing?" I yelled.

About that time Mr. Saxet walked in. The microfilm slithered across the floor and wrapped itself around his legs. With a snap, the last of the film flipped off the spool.

Mr. Saxet's eyes sort of bugged out and he waved his arms frantically. "Wha—it's you! Fenton P. Smith!" he yelled. "I might have known! You are a disaster walking on two feet! Out! Out!"

"But the film, sir. I'll— "

"No! Don't touch it! Just go!"

We didn't need to be told a second time. We scooted out of there and didn't stop until we had reached the corner. "Whew!" I breathed a sigh of relief. "I don't know why he's so touchy."

We sat down on the curb to catch our breath. I pulled the picture from the envelope and glanced at it, just to be sure I hadn't lost it in the rush.

"Holy cats!" I said, looking closer. "Gerald, would you look at that!"

Gerald studied the picture. "It looks a lot like Mac, but this is that girl cat, Cleopatra what's-her-name. All Maltese cats look alike, I think."

"No, Gerald, not the cat. Look! Look at the bracelet on that lady, Miss Collinbacher. It—it looks just like Mac's collar—see the flower design going all around her wrist? You know how eccentric rich people can be. I'll bet she had Cleopatra's collar made to match her bracelet. For the cat show, you know."

"She probably got confused and put it on Mac instead," Gerald said.

My detective-quick mind snapped into action. "Gerald, it is Mary Alice Collinbacher who needs help! We've got to save her!"

Catastasis!

"Gerald, partner," I said. "This calls for quick action on the part of the Determined Detectives."

"I think this calls for catastasis," a foghorn voice behind me bellowed.

The strong odor of lavender perfume confirmed what I already knew. I whirled around. "Mae Donna, who invited you? And besides, cata*what?*"

She stuck her nose so high in the air she'd have drowned if there were a sudden downpour of rain. "A catastasis," she said. "I do consider myself something of a word expert. Catastasis, c-a-t-a-s-t-a-s-i-s. Catastasis is intensified action," she recited. "That is what I think this case calls for—intensified action."

"But it's *our* case!" I yelled. "And we aren't calling it cata-what's-it. It's the case of the Maltese feline—that's what."

"Clever," she said, sniffing. "Call it what you want, but you are going to need all the help you can get on this one. If Mary Alice Collinbacher had to send her cat for help, that means she's incommunicado, and—"

"I thought we thought she'd be in that big old mansion," Gerald said. "What makes you think she'd be in a commu—communicado?"

I glared at dumb old Mae Donna. She didn't have to make my associate look so stupid. And I sure didn't want her to think that Fenton P. Smith didn't know a good detective word like that. "Incommunicado," I said. "I-n-c—"

"Incommunicado," Mae Donna interrupted me. "I-n-c-o-m-m-u-n-i-c-a-d-o, derives from the word communicate and means that she can't communicate, so she sent her cat to do it."

"We already decided that," I said. "The next thing we've got to do is find out who has her and why she can't communicate. When we have that, we can go to the sheriff. Then he'll listen to us. He'll have to."

"But how do we know that she's in her house?" Gerald asked. "Maybe they carried her somewhere else."

I made a face, because I hate being asked questions I can't answer. "We *don't* know for sure. But it stands to reason—her cat was not far from here. Cats don't stray more than a little way from home, do they? But even if she isn't there, maybe she left a clue. She seems pretty smart."

Gerald nodded. "So how do we get into her house?"

"Yeah, how?" Mae Donna asked.

It was nice to know that she didn't have all the answers, either. "We could disguise ourselves as exterminators," I said, "like your dad, Mae Donna."

She turned a red so bright that her skin and hair looked the same color. "Will you cut that out?" she yelled. "I wish you would just leave my father out of this."

"You're right," I conceded. "That's his cover. We'll find our own. We'll disguise ourselves as cable television repairmen. I guess you can come, too," I said to Mae Donna. "Somebody has to *bore* the bad guys with big words while we solve the case."

"Ha, ha!" Mae Donna laughed. She reached down into that big purse of hers and pulled out a skateboard. "Betcha I get my own disguise and beat you there!" she yelled, pushing off.

"Come on, Gerald," I said. "My house is closer. We can get something out of my stash of costumes. Hurry!"

We ran to my house as fast as we could and dashed into my room. I flung one costume after another out of the toy box, spotting Mac's collar. That is, Cleopatra's collar. I put it on the dresser. That reminded me.

"I better check on Mac," I said as Gerald slid into a pair of bibbed overalls that said A B C on the pocket and a blue cotton shirt. I found Mac in the closet. He had scrunched up a bunch of old socks and things and was making funny muttering noises and seemed awfully restless.

"Maybe he has a stomachache," I said. "What do you give a cat for stomachache?"

"I think they just drink water and quit eating until they feel better. That's what my dog does," Gerald said. "Is his stomach sort of rumbling or gurgling?"

I listened. "Naw," I said. "Maybe he's just bored." Just in case, though, I put down a bowl of fresh water in the closet. If that was where Mac wanted to stay, fine. Maybe he would be joining his sister Cleopatra soon. I found a pair of white dungarees and a white shirt and put them on. I grabbed my fishing tackle box from under the bed—it looked enough like a toolbox to fool someone, I figured. As a precaution, I put in a couple of false noses and painters' caps with visors that could be pulled low over our eyes.

We hurried out and jumped on my bike to get there fast. I pedaled to the red brick mansion across the street from Collinbacher Park and hid my bike in the bushes. Mae Donna was nowhere in sight. So far, so good. Gerald and I walked up to the iron gate in the high brick fence, and I rang the bell.

A guy's voice crackled over an intercom attached to the fence. "Yes?"

"We're—we're—" I spotted the letters on Gerald's overalls. "We're from the American Broadcasting Cable."

"Step in front of the surveillance camera," he demanded. He sounded mad. His voice reminded me of a growling dog—a big one. I glanced up, and sure enough, there was a little video camera bolted to the fence. When we stepped in front of it, he snarled, "The cable company? Both of you?" I don't think he believed us—not completely. I knew I was going to have to be convincing.

"Er, yes sir," I stammered.

"Then why are your uniforms different?" I had a feeling he would start barking any minute.

"Because I'm his boss," Gerald and I said at the same time.

"That is, he's my boss," we both corrected at the same time.

"Actually," a foghorn voice behind me interrupted, "I am boss to both of them. I am supervising their work for the day—so many customer complaints about their slipshod work, you know."

I turned to see Mae Donna standing there in a blue business suit and a floppy fedora hat, thick glasses, and shoes that looked three sizes too big.

I glared at her, then turned back to the camera. "We're here to check the, uh, the throttle-boggle on the cable. We're checking all of them while we're in the neighborhood."

"We don't *have* cable television," the guy growled. I couldn't stop thinking of a Doberman pinscher.

"That's why we're here," I said. "To install it. Order of Miss Mary Alice Collinbacher."

There was a sort of gurgle on the intercom, then he spoke. "But she couldn't have ordered—that is, I'm sure she didn't. You have the wrong house. Go away." This time he sounded more like a Pekinese—a high-pitched yap.

I heard the intercom click off.

We walked back toward the bikes. "Now what, Mr. Smarty?" Mae Donna said. "It's all your fault! Throttle-boggle? Of all the dumb——"

"You heard him," I interrupted her. "He said she *couldn't* have ordered cable. That means he's not *letting* her; she's incom——"

"Incommunicado," Mae Donna interrupted again. "But maybe he means she isn't there. Maybe they have taken her to some creepy old cabin deep in the woods where they don't give her any food and——"

"Never mind, Mae Donna. We get the picture," I said. "I bet she is in there. I think they'd want to keep an eye on her, keep her nearby. But even if they do have her in a creepy old cabin or in a tower on a cliff or anyplace, I bet she left us a clue in there. We just have to find it, that's all.

"So we need to get in. They don't have cable, but all these big mansions have swimming pools, don't they? We'll be pool maintenance people. Detectives on television are always getting in as pool maintenance. It's a snap."

Gerald and I exchanged shirts. I put on Mae Donna's thick glasses and one of the painters' caps. Gerald drew a quick moustache and some wrinkles on his forehead and cheeks with an eyebrow pencil Mae Donna had stashed in her big purse. Then he put on the other painters' cap. Mae Donna was wearing a pair of blue jeans rolled up under the suit, so she just took off the skirt, tied a scarf around her forehead and put on a false nose.

40

Satisfied that we looked different enough, I rang the bell again.

The intercom snapped on and the same guy, more like a pit bull this time, said, "Yeah?" The camera made a whirring sound.

I ducked my head and tried to lower my voice. "Pool men," I said.

To my relief and surprise, there was a whirring noise and the gate swung open. We scooted inside before he could change his mind.

There was no need to confront him. We kept our heads low and made our way around to the backyard. Moments later we stood facing a dirty pool, wondering how we were going to get inside the house and how we were going to save Mary Alice Collinbacher.

Catapult

"Look as if you are busy while I think," I muttered. Mae Donna picked up a skimmer and began scooping floating leaves from the pool.

Gerald bent over a big valve. "What's this?" he said, giving it a half spin.

"Don't," I warned. "That could be the pool drain valve."

There was a schlumping noise, and a pump began chugging. "Turn it back!" I said. "You'll drain the pool!" An air bubble rose to the top of the water and burst. A few leaves began circling in a whirlpool pattern.

"I can't!" Gerald yelled. "It's stuck!"

"Then find another way to look busy," I whispered. "I'm going to try and peek in a few windows to see if I can spot Miss Collinbacher."

I lifted the thick glasses and tried to see if the guy

might be spying on us, but I couldn't see anyone peeking out through the windows.

I slipped behind a tree, then dashed to a bush about midway between the pool and the house. From there I crept on my hands and knees to a bed of waist-high purple flowers. I held my breath, waiting for the yell that would surely follow if I had been spotted. Nothing. Hunched over, I skittered the last few yards to the house.

I pulled up and put my nose to a window, peering inside. I was looking at the kitchen. A man was down on his knees in the middle of the floor. He was straining at something so hard his face looked red—almost as red as Mae Donna Dockstadter's hair. He was probably the guy on the intercom. He even looked a little like a Chihuahua, now that I saw him.

A woman with hair like yellow straw was leaning over his shoulder, yelling. "You said it was going to be easy! You said we'd have the money and be out of here in a few hours! My mother said you were no good! Stupid!" She punched him on the shoulder.

"Ouch!" He swatted her hand away. "Leave me alone, will you? And don't call me stupid, Stupid! I'll never get this safe open if you stand around yammering at me. Why don't you make yourself useful for a change. See if the old broad has changed her mind about giving us the combination to this thing."

"If you were better with tools—"

I ducked back down. Mr. Dockstadter was right, as usual. There are vermin even on Collinbacher Boulevard!

At first I thought I should call the sheriff right then. But what if this guy lived there? There's no law against breaking into your own safe. I had to locate Miss Collinbacher and see if she really was the one in trouble.

Great detective that I am, I asked myself, where would somebody be kept if she were a prisoner in her own home? The answer came to me like lightning. She'd probably be kept in a bedroom, and probably on the second floor, far away from the safe they were breaking into. She probably couldn't get away from the second floor; they'd be watching the stairs. And maybe there wasn't another way out.

Of course, if the crooks had moved her, we might never find her.

"Pssssst!" Gerald said. "The pool is draining. What should I do?"

I glowered at him and put a finger to my lips to shush him. I gestured toward the house. He nodded his understanding and tiptoed back toward the pool.

As I crept around the house, I scanned the second floor windows. All except two had the drapes drawn back to let the sunshine in. I figured the closed-off windows had to be where they were holding Miss Collinbacher.

There was a tree right by one of the windows. If I could just reach the bottom limb, I could probably climb up to the window. The limb was kind of high, so I took off my belt and slung it over the top.

I pulled with all my might, and slowly the limb came toward me. Suddenly it snapped back, jerking me with it. It was like one of those catapults in the days of knights, with me as the boulder! I snatched at the branches as I was flung upward, and managed to grab hold of one.

I wiggled into a sitting position, caught my breath, then tried again to climb. Taking it one limb at a time, I managed to work my way to the window ledge. I stepped onto it. The window was open just a crack, and I pushed it up the rest of the way and peered inside. It was dark in there, and I had to wait for my eyes to adjust before climbing in.

"Hello there, young man," a soft female voice said, startling me so much I jumped and bumped my head on the window frame. "Did you come to rescue me? Thank you!"

When my heart stopped pounding, I calmed down enough to figure out the voice had to belong to the message-writer. She was certainly polite, under the circumstances. "Fenton P. Smith, ma'am." I stared into the dark and slowly made out a small figure.

In the dim light I could see that she had soft fluffy white hair, sort of like a cloud had settled over her head. Her skin was pale like tapioca pudding, and wrinkled. But her eyes seemed to glisten and dance. It was a nice face, sort of like my gramma's.

She seemed to be handcuffed to the post of a canopy bed. "Now that I know you are definitely a prisoner, I will go and get the sheriff. He'll get you out of this, Miss Collinbacher."

"Oh, please don't leave me here! Not with that chauffeur of mine, the cad! If you'll go over to the dressing table, Fenton, you will see a hat pin. I believe if you stick it in the lock hole of these cuffs you can jiggle it a bit and make them come loose."

"Yes ma'am," I said and tiptoed over to the dressing table, being careful not to bump into anything. I found the hat pin and crept back to where she was cuffed.

With my fingers, I felt for the hole on the handcuffs, then stuck the pin in—ouch! Not before sticking it in my finger, of course. I worked the pin around and around until there was a metallic click.

"Oh, thank you, Fenton," she said. "Now let's get out of here."

"But, ma'am!" I protested. "Your chauffeur is down in the kitchen. He'll see us if we use the stairs."

"Stairs?" she said. "You came in through the window, and that's how we'll go out." She eased herself out of the bed, did a few quick knee bends, and stretched out her arms, wiggling them to get her circulation back. "I've exercised the best I could, considering the confined position I've been kept in these past few days. I've just been waiting for this chance. Come on!"

She scrambled down behind me, as agile as a monkey. It was hard to believe Miss Collinbacher was old. I slipped to the ground and sort of guided her down that last drop. "My friends are in the back," I said. "I'd better get them."

"I don't believe they are in imminent danger," she said. "Let's get to a phone first, if you don't mind, of course. What is your mode of transportation, if I may ask?"

"A bike," I said.

"Then what are we waiting for?" she asked. She

scurried across the lawn as quickly as somebody my mom's age. She put her finger to her lips and pointed to a smaller iron gate in the fence, away from the camera. She pressed a button, and the gate swung open.

"One of the early Collinbachers had this little secret gate installed so he could slip in and out unnoticed. We have all used it a few times—especially when we were courting and arrived home a bit late." She chuckled. She stepped through and straightened up—she wasn't much taller than I—and breathed deeply. "Well, this is much better, I must say."

We scrambled around to where I'd hidden my bike in the bushes and she swung herself up onto the handlebars. "Let's go, young man. To a police call box, if you will."

She sat up there, pretty as you please, while I pedaled off to a police call box about three blocks away. "I certainly want to thank you for this," she said. "You are extremely brave, Fenton."

I blushed appropriately. "Aw, Gerald and I do this kind of stuff routinely. And"—I choked on the words—"Mae Donna, too."

"I certainly hated to send my dear cat out on such a mission, but I thought someone clever like you would notice the note around its neck and follow it back home."

Follow? Would Mac have eventually led us back to her house if I hadn't carried him home? It certainly would have saved a lot of time and trouble!

"There!" she said, pointing to a call box on a telephone pole. I stopped the bike. She hopped off, skittered over to the call box and told the sheriff what was going on.

"Do you want to hide out at my house until it's all over?" I asked her.

"And miss all the fun?" she said. "Certainly not! I want to see the sheriff lead that scalawag off in chains. The idea! He pranced into my life a month and four days ago, and I opened my house to him and his greedy wife. I should have suspected something when they yelled at my cat. Didn't like cats, they said. Never trust anyone who doesn't like cats, I say. They squabbled all the time like a pack of wild dogs over a morsel of food."

I grinned, remembering my own dog images. "Yes ma'am," I agreed.

"And what did they do?" she continued. "Why, two nights ago they tried to steal all my valuables while I was sleeping, and when I caught them in the act, they handcuffed me to the bed so I couldn't call the police."

She climbed back on the handlebars and continued in a calm, high-pitched voice. "They tried to force me to tell them the combination to the safe. And when I told them I was just an addled old lady who couldn't remember such things, they made me a prisoner so they could work on it at their leisure. I shall certainly fire them both immediately! And no recommendation, either."

As we pedaled back, she asked me some questions about myself. I told her about going out for baseball and finding her cat on the way home.

We arrived at the mansion just as the sheriff and his men were pulling up. Miss Collinbacher and I went through the secret gate and crept toward the pool to join Gerald and Mae Donna. About that time the back door opened and the dog-faced guy and his straw-haired wife came scrambling out of the house. She was still yelling at him and punching him on the arm. They must have seen the sheriff going in the front door, because they were leaving pretty fast.

"Don't let them get away!" I yelled. Mae Donna and Gerald made a dive for them.

"I got 'em!" Mae Donna yelled as she fell flat on her face in the grass.

"Me, too!" Gerald shouted, stumbling over Mae Donna.

The two of them were flailing around in the grass trying to get a hold on Dog Face and Straw Hair.

Their timing was off, but it was okay. Because the two crooks got their legs all tangled up with Mae Donna and Gerald and both fell headfirst into the pool, which had drained to about three feet deep by then, enough water to break their fall.

They weren't making much progress through the water, and Dog Face was yelling at Straw Hair this time. "It's all your fault! You and your stupid ideas. I told you safecracking wasn't a good idea. We could have just stuck to regular old burglary, but—"

"Just shut up before you get us into worse trouble!" Straw Hair yelled. She looked like a wrung-out floor mop. She punched him on the arm. "No ambition! That's your trouble, Stupid!" She glowered at me, Gerald and Mae Donna. "Look at them! They're nothing

50

but a bunch of kids and an old lady, Stupid, and you let them—"

Dog Face growled at her.

Dog Face and Straw Hair came up sputtering and tried to make a run for it.

Gerald and Mae Donna scrambled to their feet and headed around the pool, just in case the crooks tried to get out at the other end.

By that time the sheriff and his men were trotting out the back door, huffing and puffing. "Take them away," Miss Collinbacher said. "And good riddance."

She promised to follow the sheriff later and file a complaint of unlawful imprisonment and attempted burglary. "But first I must freshen up a bit and find Cleopatra. And then I am going to find a way to thank my friends here for rescuing me," she said.

"Cleopatra is gone, too?" I asked.

"Why, of course. I told you I had to send her off to find help," Miss Collinbacher said.

I could feel my jaw slackening. "You mean Mac is a *she?* And his—I mean her name is Cleopatra?"

"Mac?" she said.

"Engraved on his collar, his name, Mac," I said.

"Mac?" She nodded. "Oh, of course. You mean my initials in the diamond bracelet. *MAC.* Mary Alice Collinbacher."

I felt my face flush. I'd thought that was an imitation-stone cat collar, and all the time it was an expensive diamond bracelet. And Mac wasn't Mac at all, but Cleopatra.

We hung around while Miss Collinbacher freshened up. Then she got out her big old stretch limo. It was so big that we stuck the bike in the trunk and closed the lid. The three of us sat in the front seat beside her. She could barely see over the top of the steering wheel—no wonder she had a chauffeur.

You should've seen Mom's eyes pop out when we drove up in the limo and piled into the house. I introduced Miss Collinbacher and explained to Mom that she was Cleopatra's owner.

"Oh, Mac—or, Cleopatra—is quite the charmer," Mom said. "I'm glad you two have found each other, but I'll miss him—that is, her."

We tiptoed into my room to get Cleopatra and the bracelet. The diamond and ruby bracelet was on my dresser, right where I had left it. But Cleopatra was nowhere in sight. I figured she must still be in the closet. I peeked inside, and I couldn't believe my eyes! There was not one cat, but six! That is, one cat and five dark, squirming kittens.

Miss Collinbacher seemed overjoyed. "Oh, Cleopatra, my love. Your babies are truly beautiful."

Gerald knelt down beside them. "Wow!" he whispered. Wow was right! I was as proud of Mac—Cleopatra—as when she stood up to Stew.

Cleopatra left her kittens long enough to rub up against Miss Collinbacher and blink her big pumpkinlike orange eyes at her. She licked my fingers, then went back to her kittens.

Miss Collinbacher turned to Mom. "It would please Cleopatra and me," she said, "if Fenton were to have one of the kittens when they are big enough to leave home."

"You did say you were going to miss Mac," I reminded Mom.

"Well, I suppose we will be healthier and happier with one, won't we?" Mom said.

"You pick when you are ready, dear," Miss Collinbacher told me. "By the time your baseball season is over, your kitten will be ready to come home with you—sort of a victory gift."

Mae Donna sniggered. "By the time Fenton can celebrate victory, it'll be three litters later!"

I glared at her, just to let her know I planned to get even later. Then I looked at all of the kittens squirming and squealing near Cleopatra. They all looked alike. They would probably grow up to be just like Cleopatra. And I liked that idea. She was one tough cat. "I want a male," I said.

Mae Donna pushed her nose in the air. "But Cleopatra proves that the female of the cat species is certainly intelligent. Why not—"

"Because I'm naming him Mac," I said. "That's why."

"Humph," Mae Donna mumbled. "Whatever."

I touched one finger lightly to one of the tiny squirming bodies. Whichever one I chose, it'd give Mae Donna's dog a run for it. I could hardly wait!